SEEING★STARS

A Book and Poster About the Constellations

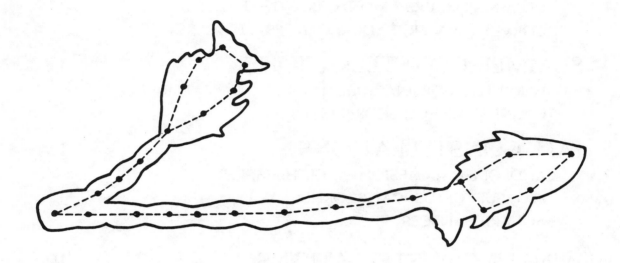

BY Barbara Seiger

COVER ILLUSTRATION AND POSTER BY
Craig Calsbeek

INTERIOR ILLUSTRATIONS BY
Cynthia Hess

Text copyright © 1993 by Barbara Seiger. Cover and poster art copyright © 1993 by Craig Calsbeek. Interior art copyright © 1993 by Grosset & Dunlap, Inc. All rights reserved. Published by Grosset & Dunlap, Inc., a member of The Putnam & Grosset Group, New York. Published simultaneously in Canada. Printed in the U.S.A.
Library of Congress Catalog Card Number: 92-43199   ISBN 0-448-40198-3   A B C D E F G H I J

CONTENTS

HOW TO USE YOUR POSTER   3

WHAT ARE CONSTELLATIONS?   4

SPRING CONSTELLATIONS   7
  URSA MAJOR, URSA MINOR, BOÖTES, DRACO,
  CORVUS, CRATER, HYDRA, CANCER, LEO, VIRGO

SUMMER CONSTELLATIONS   11
  HERCULES, CORONA BOREALIS, LYRA, SAGITTARIUS,
  CYGNUS, AQUILA, SCORPIUS, LIBRA

FALL CONSTELLATIONS   15
  ANDROMEDA, CASSIOPEIA, CEPHEUS, PERSEUS,
  PEGASUS, CETUS, CAPRICORNUS, ARIES,
  AQUARIUS, PISCES

WINTER CONSTELLATIONS   19
  ORION, LEPUS, CANIS MAJOR, CANIS MINOR,
  AURIGA, TAURUS, GEMINI

THE ZODIAC   22

The constellation maps in this book show the stars as you would see them in the early evenings from mid-northern latitudes. This region covers most of the United States, including cities as far north as Portland, Oregon; Minneapolis, Minnesota; and Augusta, Maine; and as far south as Savannah, Georgia; Fort Worth, Texas; and San Diego, California.

HOW TO USE YOUR POSTER

The star poster in the back of this book tells you which constellations to look for—and when. Just look for the months of the year around the edge of the circle. Then turn the poster so the month it is now is at the bottom. The bottom part of the poster will show you the constellations just as you would see them in the sky.

To really find these constellations in the sky, wait until it is completely dark. Then go outside where you can see the stars clearly and face south. (Watch where the sun goes down that night. Then when you go outside, face in that direction and turn to your left— you will be facing south.)

Even when you don't go outside, you can make your own starry sky with the glow-in-the-dark star stickers that also come with this book. Put the stickers on the poster to mark the stars in the constellations. The largest star sticker is for marking the special star Polaris in the very middle of the poster.

Hang your poster on your wall or ceiling so that every time you turn out the lights you can see stars!

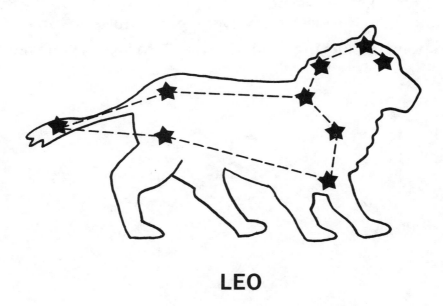

LEO

WHAT ARE CONSTELLATIONS?

Have you ever looked up at the clouds and seen shapes that remind you of animals, or even people? You can do the same thing with stars! In fact, for thousands of years that's just what stargazers have been doing. These star pictures are called **CONSTELLATIONS**.

Many constellations are named for gods and heroes of ancient myths and legends, or for animals, like **LEO** (the lion) and **TAURUS** (the bull). People also made up stories about the constellations. The names and stories helped people remember the constellations and find them in the sky. The Egyptians may have been the very first people to pick out groups of stars and name them, but most of the names and stories we remember today come from the ancient Greeks and Romans.

Today we look for constellations mostly for the fun of it. But knowing the constellations was very important to people long ago. Before clocks or calendars or compasses were invented, constellations helped people tell time and find their way in the dark.

In the daytime, you can tell if it's morning or afternoon by looking for the sun. As the earth spins, the sun seems to rise in the east every morning and set in the west every evening. So while the sun is in the east, you know it's morning. And when it's in the west, you know it's afternoon.

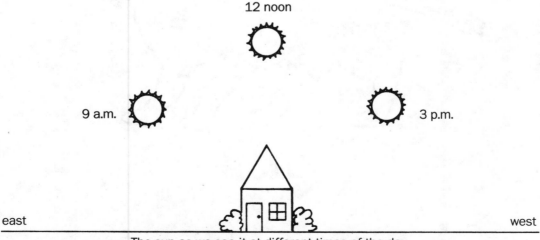

The sun as we see it at different times of the day

SPRING CONSTELLATIONS
(March–June)

On a clear spring night, these are the constellations you'll see.

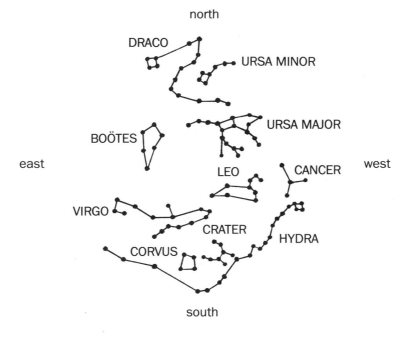

URSA MAJOR (the Great Bear)

URSA MAJOR (er-suh <u>may</u>-jer) was once a beautiful woman named Callisto, until a jealous goddess turned her into a bear. Years later, Callisto's son was hunting in the forest and almost shot the bear with his arrow. Luckily, Zeus (zoos), the king of the gods, saved Callisto by changing her son into a bear, too. Then he carried them both into the sky where they would always be safe from hunters. Now Callisto and her son form the constellations **URSA MAJOR** (the great bear) and **URSA MINOR** (the little bear).

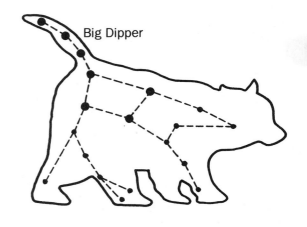

    URSA MAJOR contains the star group known as the Big Dipper.

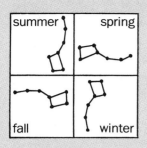

THE BIG DIPPER

The Big Dipper is made up of seven bright stars in the shape of a giant ladle. It can be seen on almost any clear night, though it changes position with the seasons.

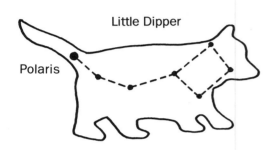

URSA MINOR (the Little Bear)

In **URSA MINOR** (er-suh <u>my</u>-ner) you'll find the famous star group we call the Little Dipper. It looks a lot like the Big Dipper but it's not quite as big or as bright. The North Star, Polaris, marks the end of the handle.

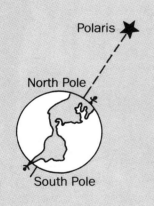

POLARIS

One special star does not move across the sky. It's called Polaris (puh-<u>lar</u>-es), or the North Star. Polaris is right above the earth's North Pole. From anywhere you look in the United States, Polaris will show you which way is north. People have used it to guide them for thousands of years.

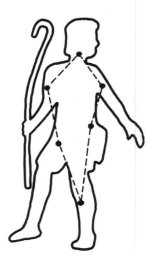

BOÖTES (the Bear Keeper)

BOÖTES (boh-<u>oh</u>-tees) invented the first plow pulled by oxen. The gods rewarded him for this clever invention with a place in the sky—with one condition: **BOÖTES** had to keep an eye on the Great Bear and Little Bear.

DRACO (the Dragon)

DRACO (<u>dray</u>-coh), or the dragon, appears in many myths and legends. It can be seen on almost any clear night between **URSA MAJOR** and **URSA MINOR**.

CORVUS (the Crow)

CORVUS (<u>core</u>-vuss), the crow, was a pet of the gods. One day they sent him to fetch some water. The crow was just about to fill his cup when he saw a fig tree and decided to stay and eat some fruit. When he finally returned, he brought a snake and told the gods that it had made him late. But the gods knew **CORVUS** was lying, and so they threw the crow, his cup, and the snake all into the sky, creating the three constellations, **CORVUS, CRATER** (the cup), and **HYDRA** (the snake).

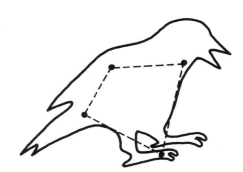

CRATER (the Cup)

Look for **CORVUS**'s cup, **CRATER** (kray-<u>ter</u>), just to the right of the crow.

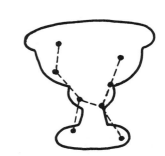

HYDRA (the Snake)

HYDRA (<u>hye</u>-druh) is the longest constellation in our sky and stretches out below **CORVUS, CRATER, CANCER, LEO,** and **VIRGO.**

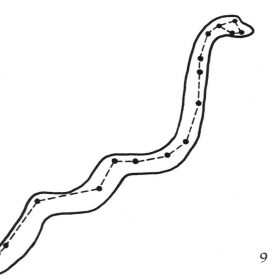

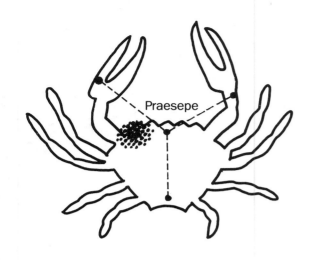

CANCER (the Crab)

CANCER (<u>can</u>-ser), the crab, was a favorite pet of the gods. Once when the gods were mad at the Greek hero Hercules, they sent the magic crab to pinch him. But Hercules was so strong that he tossed the crab into the sky.

In the left arm of **CANCER** is a misty patch of stars called Praesepe (pray-<u>see</u>-pee), or "the Beehive." If you cannot see Praesepe, there's a good chance that it will rain soon—even a little bit of water vapor in the air will hide these stars.

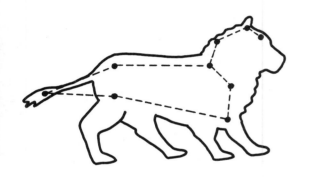

LEO (the Lion)

LEO (<u>lee</u>-oh) was a mighty lion who roamed the countryside of ancient Greece killing any creature that came in its path. Its skin was so tough that no weapon could pierce it. Because the gods admired the fierce lion they honored **LEO** with a place in the zodiac.

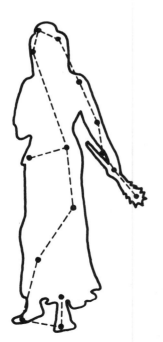

VIRGO (the Maiden)

VIRGO (<u>ver</u>-go) is Persephone (per-<u>sef</u>-uh-nee), the daughter of the goddess of the earth. She was married to the king of the underworld, but still returns to earth to spend half of every year with her mother. To this day, when Persephone is in the underworld, the earth goddess is sad and lets nothing grow. But when Persephone returns, her mother rejoices and the earth comes to life. And so, said the Greeks, we have winter and summer.

SUMMER CONSTELLATIONS
(June–September)

On a clear summer night, look for these constellations.

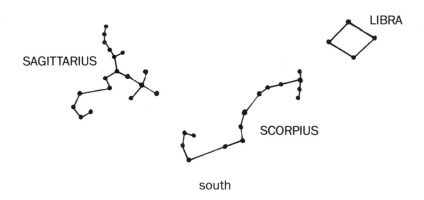

north

CYGNUS   LYRA   HERCULES

CORONA BOREALIS

AQUILA

east   west

LIBRA

SAGITTARIUS

SCORPIUS

south

HERCULES (the Strong Man)

HERCULES (<u>her</u>-kew-lees) was famous in ancient Greece for his amazing strength, and he is the star of many ancient legends.

Look for a hazy patch of light just to **HERCULES**'s side—it is really thousands of tightly grouped stars.

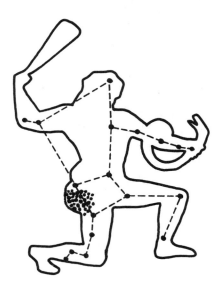

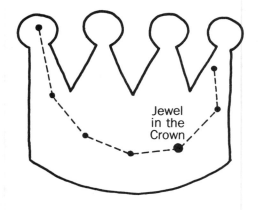

CORONA BOREALIS
(the Northern Crown)

CORONA BOREALIS (cuh-<u>roh</u>-nuh bore-ee-<u>al</u>-us) is the crown that once belonged to a princess in ancient Greece. It was given to her by a young god who fell madly in love with her. The couple lived happily for many years, until the princess died. Then the god set her crown among the stars to remember her by.

The brightest of the seven stars which make up the constellation is sometimes called "the Jewel in the Crown."

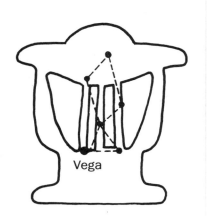

LYRA (the Harp)

LYRA (<u>lye</u>-ruh) is named for the harp of the famous Greek musician Orpheus (<u>or</u>-fee-us).

LYRA is easy to find because it contains Vega (<u>vay</u>-guh), the brightest star in the summer sky. You can find this star almost directly overhead.

SAGITTARIUS (the Archer)

SAGITTARIUS (saj-uh-<u>tair</u>-ee-us) was a centaur, a creature with the head and upper body of a man and the lower body of a horse. **SAGITTARIUS** was the archery instructor of all the Greek heroes. One day in archery practice a student accidentally shot the centaur with a poisoned arrow. Because he was immortal, the wound could not kill **SAGITTARIUS**, but it was so painful that he begged the gods to let him die. The gods finally granted him his wish and gave **SAGITTARIUS** a comfortable place to rest in the sky.

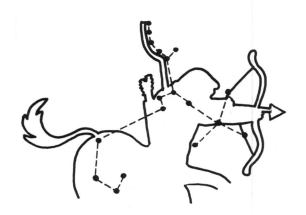

CYGNUS (the Swan)

CYGNUS (<u>sig</u>-nus) was the best friend of Phaethon (<u>fay</u>-uh-tun), the son of the sun god. One day Phaethon persuaded his father to let him drive the sun chariot across the sky. But the small boy could not control the horses. The chariot swooped down so close to the earth that the gods were afraid the whole earth would be burned. So they stopped Phaethon by flinging him into the ocean. **CYGNUS** swam back and forth with his head underwater searching for Phaethon. But he never found his friend. Finally, the gods took pity on **CYGNUS** and changed him into a swan. Later they placed him among the stars.

The six brightest stars in **CYGNUS** form a cross known as the Northern Cross.

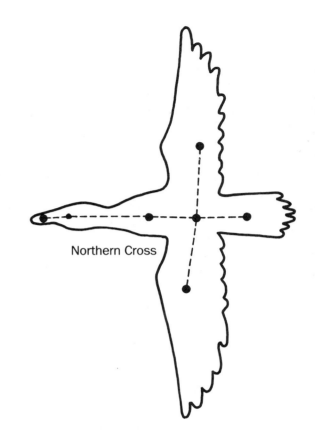

Northern Cross

AQUILA (the Eagle)

AQUILA (<u>ack</u>-will-uh), the eagle, was a favorite pet and messenger of the gods. When the gods needed a new servant, they sent **AQUILA** to earth to find one. The eagle searched until he found a handsome prince named Ganymede (<u>gan</u>-ee-meed), who soon became the gods' favorite servant. To reward **AQUILA** for his excellent choice they gave the eagle a place in the sky. After his death, Ganymede himself was placed in another part of the sky, as the constellation **AQUARIUS**.

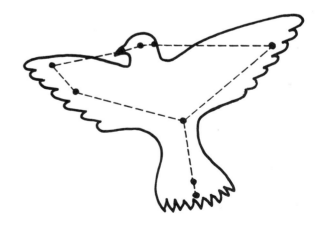

SCORPIUS (the Scorpion)

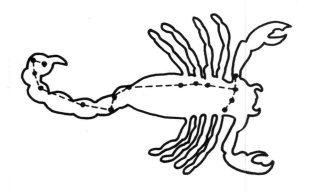

The giant scorpion **SCORPIUS** (<u>scor</u>-pee-us) was sent by the gods to punish the haughty hunter **ORION**, who boasted that he could kill all the animals in the world. **SCORPIUS** stung **ORION** and killed him and was rewarded by the gods with a place in the sky. The gods made **ORION** into a constellation as well, but because they were enemies, **ORION** and **SCORPIUS** are never seen in the sky at the same time.

Look for a reddish star right in the heart of **SCORPIUS**.

LIBRA (the Scales)

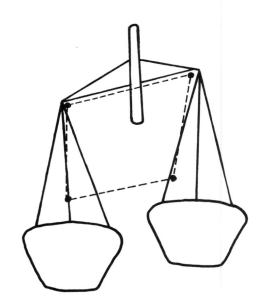

The constellation **LIBRA** (<u>lee</u>-bruh) is made up of stars which once marked the claws of the scorpion, **SCORPIUS**. Many years ago, astrologers decided that these stars should make up their own constellations.

LIBRA is represented by a pair of balanced scales. Not surprisingly, this sign of the zodiac is associated with balance, harmony, and peace.

FALL CONSTELLATIONS
(September–December)

If you look at the sky on a clear fall night, these are the constellations you'll see. Almost all of them are connected to the famous myth of **ANDROMEDA**.

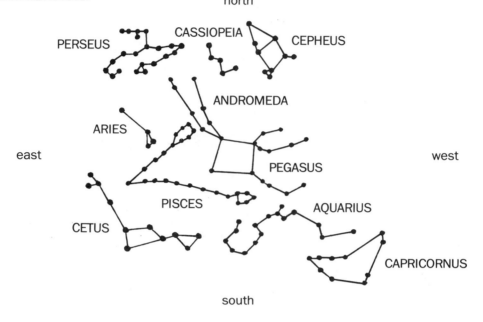

The Andromeda Story

ANDROMEDA was the beautiful daughter of the king and queen of Ethiopia. **ANDROMEDA**'s mother bragged that she was even more beautiful than the goddesses of the sea. But when the goddesses heard this they were furious and asked Poseidon (puh-<u>side</u>-un), the god of the sea, for revenge. So Poseidon sent a great sea monster named **CETUS** to swim along the shores of the kingdom devouring everyone he could. Horrified, **ANDROMEDA**'s father begged Poseidon to stop the monster. But the sea god told the king that the only way to save his people was to give **ANDROMEDA** to the monster. With no other choice, the king sadly chained his daughter to a rock by the sea and left her there. Luckily for **ANDROMEDA**, the hero **PERSEUS** happened to be riding by on his flying horse, **PEGASUS**. He bravely killed the sea monster, and carried the beautiful princess away.

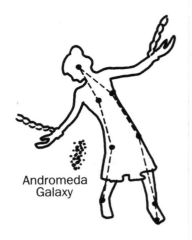

ANDROMEDA (the Chained Maiden)

ANDROMEDA (an-<u>dram</u>-ed-uh) sits in the sky chained to her rock. On a very clear, dark night look for a glowing patch of light near **ANDROMEDA**'s right side. This is the Andromeda Galaxy, a group of more than 200 billion stars!

Andromeda Galaxy

CASSIOPEIA (Andromeda's Mother)

CASSIOPEIA (cass-ee-uh-<u>pee</u>-uh) forms an easy-to-recognize "M" or "W" in the sky, depending on the season.

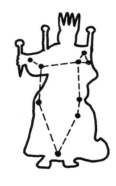

CEPHEUS (Andromeda's Father)

CEPHEUS (<u>see</u>-fee-us) sits to the right of his wife.

PERSEUS (the Hero)

PERSEUS (<u>per</u>-see-us), **ANDROMEDA**'s hero, stands near her. He holds the head of Medusa (meh-<u>doo</u>-suh), a hideous monster whose hair was made of living snakes. **PERSEUS** destroyed the monster before he rescued **ANDROMEDA**.

PEGASUS (the Winged Horse)

PEGASUS (peg-uh-sus) is pictured flying across the sky. A group of four stars called the Great Square makes up the horse's wing.

Scheat (shee-ott), the star which marks **PEGASUS**'s chest, is one of the largest stars we know of. It's so big that if it were as close to the earth as the sun is, it would take up almost all of our sky.

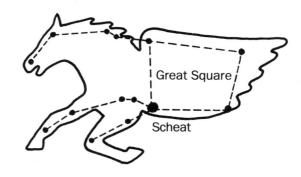

CETUS (the Sea Monster)

CETUS (seet-us) is pictured as a whale—which for a long time people believed to be a kind of sea monster.

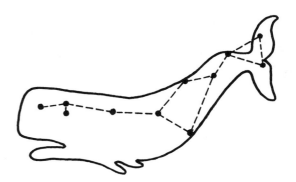

CAPRICORNUS (the Sea Goat)

CAPRICORNUS (cap-ri-corn-us) was a god, until he changed himself into a half-goat, half-fish in order to escape from a monster. In his new form, the gods raised him into the sky as the constellation **CAPRICORNUS**.

ARIES (the Ram)

ARIES (air-ees) was a magic ram, known in ancient Greece for his golden fleece, and for rescuing a young prince who was in danger of being murdered. **ARIES** was rewarded by the gods with a special place in the sky.

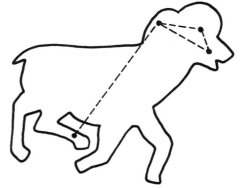

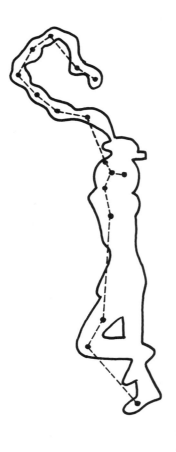

AQUARIUS (the Water Carrier)

AQUARIUS (uh-<u>kwair</u>-ee-us) is a symbol of luck and represents the gods' servant, Prince Ganymede. He carries a jug of water which he pours onto the earth.

PISCES (the Fishes)

PISCES (<u>pie</u>-sees) represents the Greek goddess of love and beauty, Aphrodite (af-ruh-<u>dite</u>-ee), and her son, Eros (<u>eer</u>-oss). One day while walking along a river, Aphrodite and Eros were attacked by a monster. To escape, they jumped into the water, changed into fish, and swam away. The gods remembered this story by placing the images of the two fish in the sky as constellations.

The two fish of **PISCES** are joined by a bright star in the middle of the constellation.

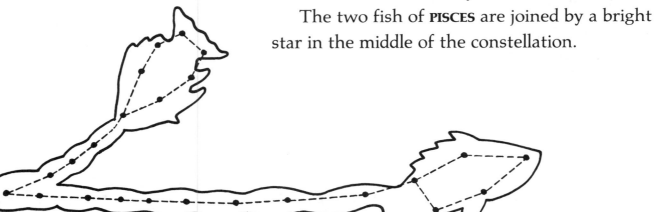

WINTER CONSTELLATIONS
(December–March)

During the winter months, these are the constellations to look for.

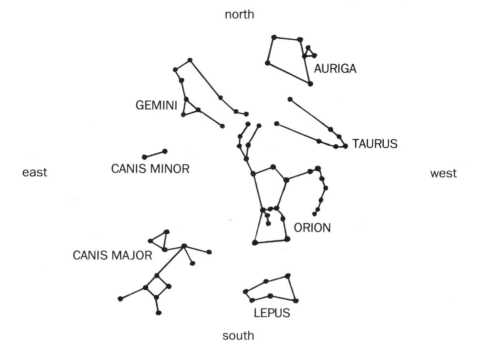

north

AURIGA

GEMINI

TAURUS

east   CANIS MINOR   west

ORION

CANIS MAJOR

LEPUS

south

ORION (the Great Hunter)

ORION (uh-<u>rye</u>-un) was a famous hunter who bragged that he could kill all the animals in the world. The gods decided to teach the hunter a lesson by sending the giant scorpion, **SCORPIUS**, to sting **ORION** while he was hunting a hare. Then, as an example to all mortals, the gods placed **ORION, LEPUS** (the hare), **CANIS MAJOR** and **CANIS MINOR** (**ORION**'s hunting dogs), and **SCORPIUS** in the sky as constellations.

    ORION is one of the easiest constellations to find in the winter sky. In fact, because it is directly over the earth's equator, it can be seen from any place on earth.

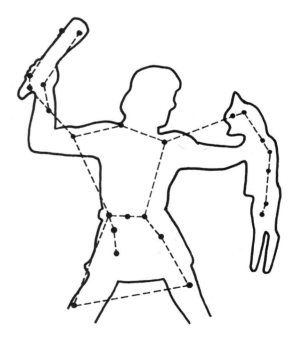

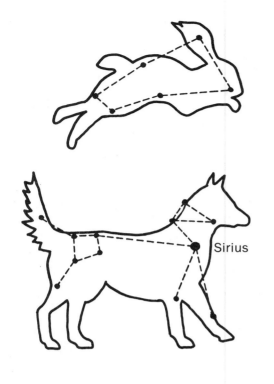

LEPUS (the Hare)

LEPUS (<u>leep</u>-us) is a small constellation and is found almost directly beneath **ORION**.

Sirius

CANIS MAJOR (the Great Dog)

CANIS MAJOR (<u>kay</u>-ness <u>may</u>-jer) is easy to find because the dog's collar contains the very brightest star in the night sky. It is called Sirius (<u>see</u>-ree-us), or "the Dog Star."

CANIS MINOR (the Little Dog)

Just across the Milky Way from **CANIS MAJOR** is its little brother, **CANIS MINOR** (<u>kay</u>-ness <u>mye</u>-ner).

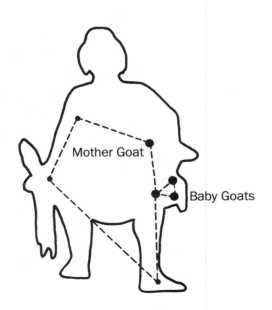

Mother Goat

Baby Goats

AURIGA (the Charioteer)

AURIGA (aw-<u>rye</u>-guh) was the first man to harness four horses to a chariot. The gods rewarded him for this important invention with a place of honor in the sky.

   AURIGA holds the reins to his chariot in his right hand. In his left arm he carries a small goat, marked by one bright star known as "the Mother Goat." Just below "the Mother Goat" is a triangle of three smaller stars called "the Baby Goats."

TAURUS (the Bull)

TAURUS (<u>tor</u>-us) is the great white bull which the god Zeus changed himself into in order to meet a beautiful princess. The princess loved animals, and liked the bull so much that she got on his back for a ride. As soon as she did, **TAURUS** jumped into the river and swam away with her.

TAURUS is pictured swimming with only his head and front feet visible above the water. A V-shaped group of stars called Hyades (<u>hye</u>-uh-deez) outlines his nose. A star cluster called the Pleiades (<u>plee</u>-uh-deez) marks his left shoulder.

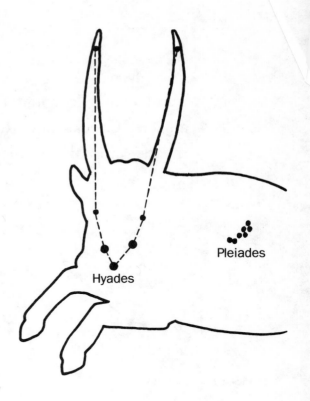

Pleiades

Hyades

GEMINI (the Twins)

GEMINI (<u>jem</u>-uh-nye) represents the twins Castor (<u>kas</u>-ter) and Pollux (<u>pall</u>-ucks). The brothers were so close that when one died the other begged Zeus to let him die, too, so he could be with his brother again. Zeus finally decided to place the brothers together in the sky to reward them for their faithfulness. Then he set a special bright star in each one's head.

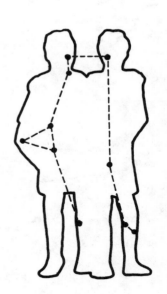

THE ZODIAC

Twelve of the constellations form a circle around the sun. The ancient Greeks and Romans called the circle the **ZODIAC**—which means "animal circle."

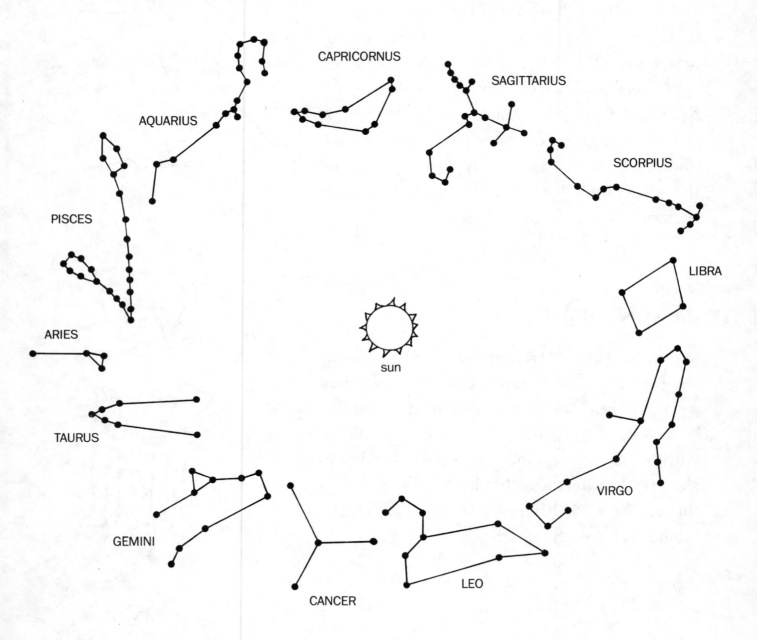

Astrologers believe that the day you were born determines which constellation will be your "sign of the zodiac." They also believe that your sign can tell a lot about what kind of person you are.

BIRTHDAY	ZODIAC SIGN	CHARACTERISTICS
Jan. 20–Feb. 18	AQUARIUS (the Water Carrier)	curious, outgoing
Feb. 19–March 20	PISCES (the Fishes)	artistic, sensitive
March 21–April 19	ARIES (the Ram)	brave, energetic
April 20–May 20	TAURUS (the Bull)	affectionate, faithful
May 21–June 20	GEMINI (the Twins)	talkative, smart
June 21–July 22	CANCER (the Crab)	emotional, patriotic
July 23–Aug. 22	LEO (the Lion)	proud, playful
Aug. 23–Sept. 22	VIRGO (the Maiden)	modest, neat
Sept. 23–Oct. 22	LIBRA (the Scales)	friendly, peaceful
Oct. 23–Nov. 21	SCORPIUS (the Scorpion)	secretive, intense
Nov. 22–Dec. 21	SAGITTARIUS (the Archer)	generous, restless
Dec. 22–Jan. 19	CAPRICORNUS (the Sea Goat)	ambitious, realistic

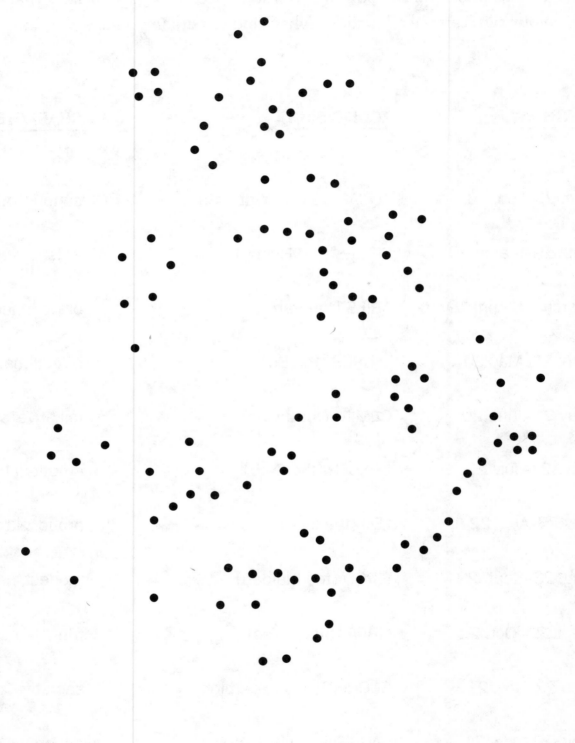

Here is a picture of the night sky in spring. Just for fun, see if you can pick out all the constellations.